Corey R. Tabor

Mel Fell

BALZER + BRAY
An Imprint of HarperCollinsPublishers

One day, when Mama was away, Mel decided it was time to learn to fly. She had been in the nest long enough.

"Aren't you scared?" asked her sister, Pim.

"Yes," said Mel. "But I won't let that stop me."

She looked down.

"It sure is a long drop," said her brother, Pip.

"Well," said Mel, "I've got wings."

Mel *was* scared and it was a long drop, but today was the day she would fly.

"See you soon!" she told her siblings. She jumped. She flipped. She spread her wings. And then . . . .

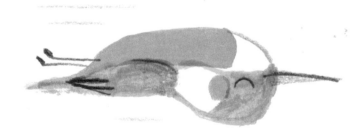

she fell.

Mel fell and fell.

The squirrels tried to catch her. They really did. They'd grown quite fond of those squeaky little chirpers upstairs.

Aieeeeee!

But it was no use. They
missed her by a whisker.

"Zzeezill zzayzzoo!"*
said the bees.
But they barely
slowed her down.

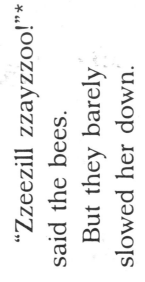

*"We will save you!"

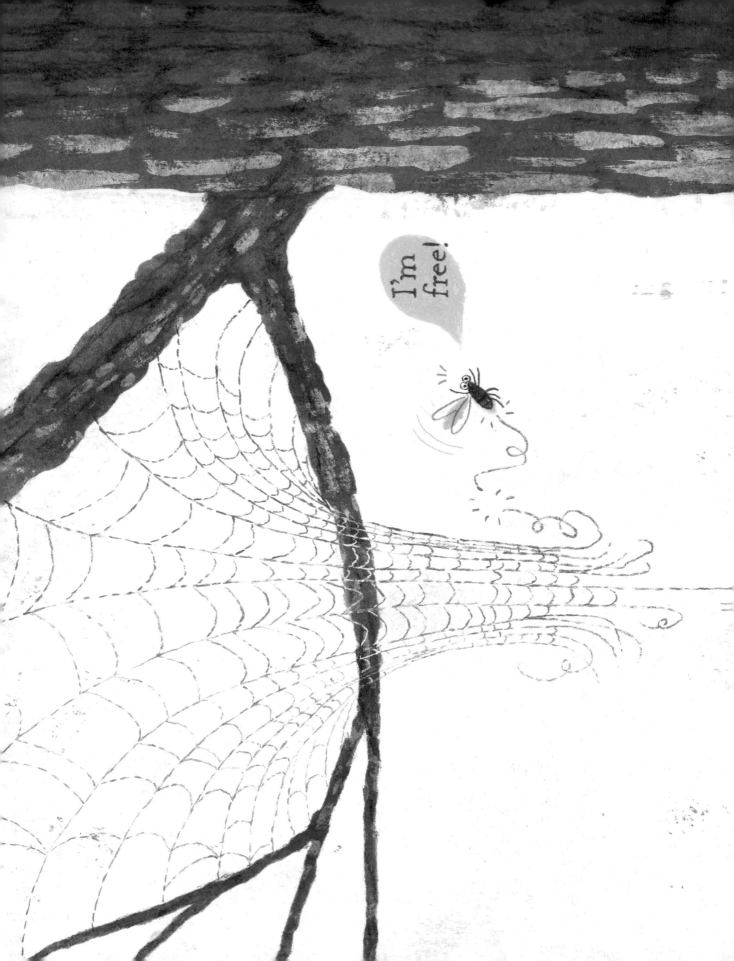

Even the spider lent a
hand. (Eight of them.)

But still, Mel fell.

Do…not…fear,…
helpless…little…
bird,…I…will…
catch…you…!

She fell and fell.

Oh no!

She snapped her beak and caught a fat little fish.

turn the book!

Mel dived into the water.

She kicked her legs.
She wiggled her tail feathers.
She spread her wings. And then . . . .

this way →

She flew!

Mel flew and flew.

As Mel flew by, the
spider clapped her hands.
All eight of them.

clap
clap
clap

The bees said,
"Huzzzzah! Huzzzzah!"

The squirrels raced
her to the top.

Mama was waiting when
she got there.
"I flew! I flew!" said Mel.

"I knew you could!" said Mama.
"I knew I could, too," said Mel.

Do...not...fear...
helpless...little...
fish...I...will...
catch...you...!

SPLASH

AUTHOR'S NOTE

Mel is a kingfisher. Kingfishers catch fish by diving into the water from tree branches or wires. Many kingfishers nest in tunnels they dig in earthen banks near water, while others nest in tree hollows (some even live in old termite nests). A young kingfisher probably doesn't catch a fish the first time they leave the nest. But then, Mel is a very special bird.

For Mandy and Will

ISBN 978-0-06-287801-4

The artist used pencil, colored pencil, and acrylic paint, assembled digitally, to create the illustrations for this book. Typography by Dana Fritts

22 23 24 PC 10 9 8 7 6 ❖ First Edition